THE GOLDEN FLOWER

A TAINO MYTH FROM PUERTO RICO

by NINA JAFFE illustrated by ENRIQUE O. SÁNCHEZ

Simon & Schuster Books for Young Readers

SIMON & SCHUSTER BOOKS FOR YOUNG READERS
An imprint of Simon & Schuster Children's Publishing Division
1230 Avenue of the Americas
New York, New York 10020
SIMON & SCHUSTER BOOKS FOR YOUNG READERS is a trademark of Simon & Schuster.
Designed by Lucille Chomowicz
The text of this book is set in 14 point Stone Sans.
The illustrations were done in acrylic and gouache.
Printed and bound in the United States of America.
First Edition
10 9 8 7 6 5 4 3 2 1
Library of Congress Cataloging-in-Publication Data:
Jaffe, Nina. The Golden Flower: A Taino Myth from Puerto Rico / retold by Nina Jaffe ;
illustrated by Enrique O. Sánchez. — 1st ed.
p. cm.
Summary: This myth explains the origin of the sea, the forest,
and the island now called Puerto Rico.
ISBN: 0-689-80469-5
1. Taino Indians—Legends. 2. Tales—Puerto Rico. [1. Taino Indians—Legends.
2. Indians of the West Indies—Puerto Rico—Legends. 3. Creation—Folklore. 4. Folklore—Puerto Rico.]
I. Sánchez, Enrique O., ill. II. Title.
F1969.J33 1996 398.2'097295—dc20 [E] 92-42364

For Dania Vázquez—dear friend, gifted teacher—amiga de mi corazón.
—N. J.

For my editor, Soyung Pak
—E. O. S.

The author gratefully acknowledges Otilio Diaz, director of La Casa de La Herencia Puertorriqueña in New York City, who reviewed the text for historical and linguistic accuracy and detail. Special thanks are also due to Mari Haas at Teacher's College, Columbia University, for her support and encouragement.

Long ago, the island of Puerto Rico was called *Boriquén.* This was the name given to it by the first people who lived there, the Taino. From time to time, the families in a Taino village would stop their work and gather together for a celebration called an *areito.* All through the night, they would dance and sing. Then young and old would gather together in a great circle and listen to stories of magic and wonder, of Taino heroes, and of how things came to be.

As you read this book, imagine that you, too, are sitting in this magic circle on a warm tropical night. The wind is blowing through the palm trees, the stars twinkle in the sky, and the storyteller begins to weave an ancient myth, a Taino tale from long ago. . . .

In the beginning of the world, there was no water anywhere on earth. There was only a tall mountain that stood alone on a wide desert plain.

There were no green plants. There were no flowers. All the people lived on top of this mountain.

One day, a child went walking on the dry land below the mountain. As he bent down over the ground looking for food, something floated by on the wind. He reached out and caught it in his hand. It was a seed. A small, brown seed. He put the seed into his pouch.

The next day, he went walking, and again found something as it floated by on the wind. It was another seed. Day by day, he gathered these seeds until his pouch was full. It could not hold anymore. And the child said to himself, "I will plant these seeds at the top of our mountain."

He planted the seeds and waited. One morning, a tiny green leaf appeared. The child watched. From under the ground, a forest began to grow high on top of the mountain.

All the people came to see. It was a forest of many-colored flowers, a magic garden of green leaves and thick branches. The child was happy.

In the middle of the forest, at the foot of the tallest tree, there grew a vine that wrapped itself around the tree.

And from that vine there grew a flower more beautiful than all
the rest. A bright flower with golden petals.

And from that flower, something new appeared in the forest.
It looked like a little ball. "Look!" cried the child. "Something is
growing out of the flower!"

As the people gathered around to watch, the ball grew larger and larger, until it became a great yellow globe that shone like the sun. Even as they walked on the dry land far below, people could see it shining on top of the mountain.

One woman said, "If you put your ear next to the ball, you can
hear strange noises coming from inside." The people listened.
Strange sounds and murmuring could be heard. But nobody
knew what was hidden inside.

The people were afraid. After that, they all stayed away. Even the child stayed away.

One day, a man walking on the desert plain saw the golden ball. He said, "If that shining ball were mine, I would have the power of the sun. I could light up the sky, or make darkness fall." And he ran toward it, climbing up the rocky mountainside.

On the other side of the mountain, another man saw the shining globe, and he also said, "I want that thing for myself. It will give me great powers." He, too, began to run. Each one climbed quickly. Each one found a footpath that led to the tree.

They both ran without stopping until they reached the
shining globe at the same time. But what they found was not
really a ball; it was the fruit of the golden flower: a *calabaza*—
a pumpkin.

The two men began to fight and argue.
"It is mine!" said one.
"No, it is mine!" said the other.
Each man grabbed the pumpkin. They pushed and pulled. They
pulled and tugged until . . .

. . . finally, the vine broke. The pumpkin began to roll down the mountain faster and faster, until it crashed into a sharp rock and burst apart.

Whoosh! Waves of water poured out of the pumpkin. The water bubbled and foamed. The waves began to cover the earth, flooding the desert plain, rising higher and higher.

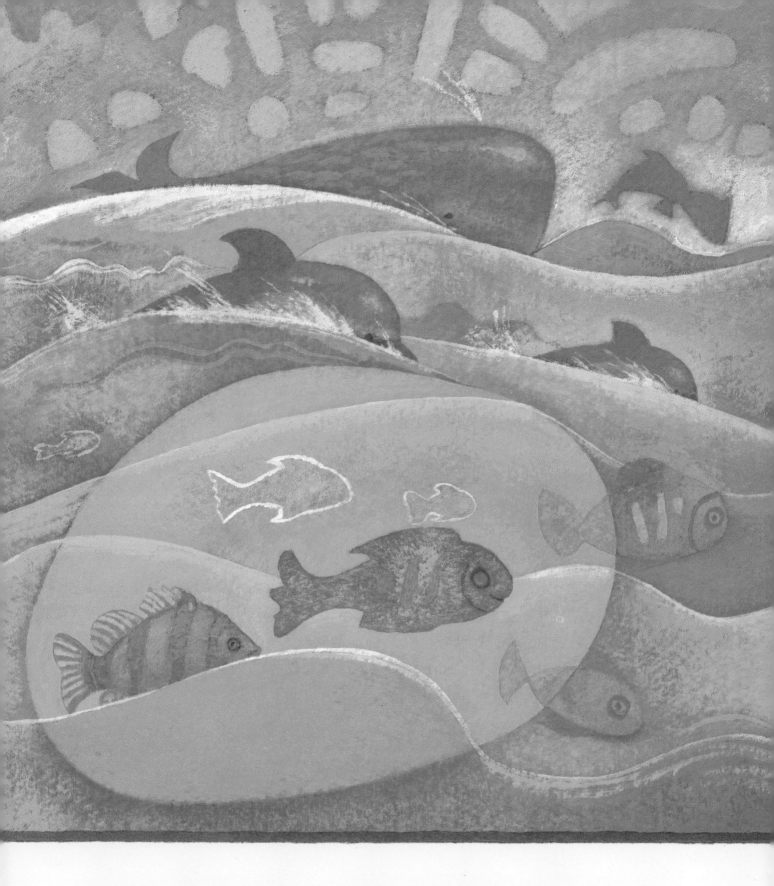

For it was the sea that had been hidden inside the pumpkin.
Out came the creatures: whales, dolphins, crabs, and sunfish. All
the people ran to the top of the mountain to hide in the forest
of green leaves.

"Will the whole earth be covered?" they cried.
Higher and higher the waters kept rising, up the sides of
the mountain.

But when the water reached the edge of the magic forest the little boy had planted, it stopped.

The people peeked out from behind the leaves. And what did they see? Small streams running through the trees. A beach of golden sand. And the wide open ocean, sparkling all around them.

Now the people could drink from the cool streams and splash in the rippling waves. Now they could gather fish from the flowing tides and plant their crops.

The child laughed and sang as the sun shone down and
breezes blew through the green leaves and rustled the many-
colored flowers. Water had come to the earth!

And that is how, the Taino say, between the sun and the
sparkling blue sea, their island home—Boriquén—came to be.

AFTERWORD

I first encountered this magical tale of the Taino people in a Spanish text by Carmen Puigdollers.* I began to retell it in schools and libraries. In 1993, Lilian Ayala, a teacher in New York City, told me that she remembered hearing her mother tell this same story at family gatherings when she was a child in Puerto Rico. In my research, I learned that stories in which the sea was hidden inside a pumpkin *(calabaza)* were common among many of the native cultures in South America and the Caribbean.

The Taino called their island home Boriquén (bo-ree-KEN), which means "land of the brave lord." They were a peaceful people who survived by hunting and fishing in the rich tropical forests and planting in their own fields. Their houses, called *bohios* (bo-EE-ohs), were made of wood and cane roofed with straw. The Taino chief was called a *cacique* (kah-SEE-kay), and it was he who told the myths and legends during the *areito* (ah-RAY-toh) ceremonies.

After Columbus landed his ships on the island's shore in 1493, the Spaniards conquered Boriquén. The Taino were enslaved. Most of them died. Despite the destruction of their people, many words in Puerto Rico today come from the Taino language. Taino foods are still cooked, Taino instruments are still played, and Puerto Ricans still proudly call their island "Borinquen" in honor of the Taino heritage that is such an important part of their history and culture.

*Puigdollers, Carmen. "Como se formó la bella isla de Borinquen" in *Presencia Taina*. Cambridge, MA, National Assessment and Dissemination Center, Lesley College, 1979.